Copyright © 2024 Kate Pricklewood
All rights reserved.
ISBN: 978-1-0685583-0-6

The Hedgehog Family's Forest Adventure

Kate Pricklewood

Once upon a time, in a cozy little burrow on the edge of a great forest, there lived a very happy hedgehog family. The family was small but full of love (and prickles!).

There was Daddy Hedgehog, who was strong and wise (but always forgot where he put his glasses), Mommy Hedgehog, who was kind and caring (and made the best nut bread in the whole forest), and their three children—Holly, Henry, and Hazel — who were prickly, curious, and always full of questions... lots and lots of questions!

One bright morning, the hedgehog family decided it was the perfect day for an adventure. So, they packed some berries, a small jar of honey, and a loaf of Mommy's famous nut bread (with an extra pinch of love, of course).

Daddy Hedgehog tried to pack his glasses too, but... he lost them again. "Where could they be?"
Just as they were about to leave, Holly giggled and pointed, "Daddy, aren't those your glasses on top of your head?"
Daddy Hedgehog chuckled, feeling a bit silly. "Ah, so they are! I guess I'm all set now!" he said, adjusting them with a grin.

"Onward!" Daddy Hedgehog cheered, pretending to be a brave explorer. "To the heart of the forest!"

As they waddled through the leafy path, the little hedgehogs squealed with joy at everything they saw. "Look!" cried Hazel, pointing at a cluster of mushrooms. "They're HUGE! Are they magic? Can we ride them?"

Henry stopped to sniff some flowers and sneezed. "ACHOO! I think the flowers are tickling my nose!"

Meanwhile, Holly was busy chasing a butterfly, but she kept bumping into bushes. "I'll catch you!" she giggled, "If you ever fly in a straight line!"

Soon, the family came to a clearing in the woods where they saw a tall deer grazing quietly. The deer looked up, smiling at the small hedgehog family. "Hello there," said the deer in a gentle voice. "What brings you to the forest today?"

"We're on an adventure!" said Henry excitedly. "And so far, I've been tickled by flowers, and Holly's been chasing a butterfly that's much faster than she is!"

The deer chuckled softly. "Well, you certainly sound like adventurers! I would love to join you little hedgehogs, but today is a special day for my family. We are having a big reunion to celebrate Grandma Deer's birthday. But I do know a wise owl who lives in a big oak tree ahead. He's always full of advice... though he tells the longest bedtime stories!"

"Maybe we'll ask him to skip to the ending," whispered Holly, giggling.

The hedgehogs thanked the deer and continued their journey. As they approached the old oak tree, they heard a soft hooting sound. "Whoooo's there?" came a voice from the branches above.
"It's the Hedgehog family!" Holly called out, cupping her paws around her mouth like a megaphone.

The wise owl swooped down from a low branch, feathers puffed up and full of wisdom. He blinked his big, sparkling eyes. "Welcome, little hedgehogs! Now, don't worry, I won't bore you with too many wise words... this time. How about I show you a secret pond instead? All the cool animals hang out there."

"Cool animals?" Henry said, eyes wide. "Do you mean... penguins?!"

"No penguins, I'm afraid," the owl chuckled. "But we do have some very playful ducks!"

The hedgehogs followed the owl through the trees, giggling as they went. Soon, they heard the sound of water splashing. When they reached the pond, they saw squirrels chasing each other through the trees, rabbits hopping around, and ducks having a splashing contest in the water.

Hazel gasped. "Look! Squirrels, rabbits, and... *flying penguins*!"

The owl giggled, "Flying penguins! Oh, Hazel, those are ducks! If penguins took to the skies, they'd probably need parachutes!"

As the hedgehog family waddled closer to the pond, they marveled at the bustling forest life. Squirrels were zooming around like little forest acrobats, but what really caught the hedgehogs' attention was a lively group of rabbits by the water, laughing and playing hopscotch.

Henry waddled up to them shyly, his spines quivering with excitement. "Hello!" he said, "Do you… hop for fun?"
One of the rabbits turned around and winked. "Of course! And we're professionals. Want to try? We're also the hide-and-seek champions of the forest!"

Soon, the hedgehogs and rabbits were playing hide-and-seek together. Every time a rabbit found a hedgehog hiding behind a bush, they all burst into laughter. "You're so prickly, it's like finding a cactus!" said one of the rabbits with a twitch of its nose.

Meanwhile, Holly waddled closer to the water where the ducks were having their splash party. One curious duckling swam over, quacking cheerfully. "Hello, little hedgehog! Do you like to swim?" it asked with a playful tilt of its head.

The hedgehog chuckled, dipping a leg in the water. "We don't swim much… but wow, this water is *ticklish*!"
The mother duck waddled over with a smile. "You're welcome to join us any time by the pond," she said warmly.

The rabbits, ducks, and hedgehogs spent the whole afternoon together, laughing, splashing, and playing hopscotch. They even shared some of Mommy Hedgehog's nut bread, which was declared the tastiest bread in the forest (after some very serious taste-testing, of course).

"Wow!" said Hazel, her eyes sparkling with joy. "This is the BEST adventure EVER!"

As the sun began to set, casting a golden glow over the peaceful forest, the hedgehog family waddled back to their cozy burrow, full of stories to tell and new friends to remember.

"I can't wait to go back and visit everyone," said Holly, yawning sleepily.
"Me too" agreed Henry, snuggling close to his mother.
Daddy Hedgehog smiled. "And next time, we'll bring even more nut bread to share with all our friends! And maybe….we can even find out if those mushrooms really are magic!"

With that, the little hedgehog family snuggled up in their burrow, dreaming of more silly, splashy adventures to come.

Daddy Hedgehog

Daddy Hedgehog is the sturdy and wise head of the family, always ready to lead his little hedgehogs on new adventures. His curiosity makes him a bit forgetful, especially when it comes to his glasses, which are often misplaced. With his playful imagination, he loves pretending to be a brave explorer, even though he's known for getting lost in his own backyard.

Mommy Hedgehog

Mommy Hedgehog is the heart of the family, always nurturing her little ones with love and delicious nut bread. She's tall and graceful, with a warm smile that can make even the darkest forest seem cozy. Whether she's packing picnics or offering gentle advice, her caring nature keeps the family safe and happy on all their woodland adventures.

Holly

The eldest of the hedgehog siblings, Holly is the most thoughtful and cautious. She's always asking questions and thinking deeply about everything they encounter in the forest. Holly loves organizing their adventures and ensuring everyone sticks together.

Henry

Henry is the adventurous middle child, full of energy and always ready to climb the tallest trees or jump into any adventure. He's fearless, curious, and often the first to notice the magic in the forest, like hidden ponds or mysterious trails. Henry's boundless enthusiasm keeps the family on their toes, and his bravery makes every adventure a little more exciting.

Hazel

The youngest of the family, Hazel is a bundle of joy and laughter. Her wide-eyed wonder at the world around her lights up their adventures, and she has a knack for finding the beauty in every little thing, like sparkling mushrooms or a secret pond.